Adventures in Space

by
Juanita Webber

Watermill Press

Printed in the United States of America

Illustrations by Thomas Heggie

ISBN 0-89375-806-X

Contents

Instant Jungle   5

A Deadly Shower   18

Field Trip   29

Home Run, Three Miles   41

Cosmic Net   53

Planet of Stone   63

Green Doctor   74

New Earth   85

Instant Jungle

Jacob and Diana peered through the thick windows of their spaceship. Ahead was a tiny, smooth planet. It seemed almost white against the empty blackness of space.

"Check the map again," Diana told her partner. She steered the spaceship in for a closer look.

Jacob pressed a series of buttons before him. A map of the area flashed upon a dark screen. He stared at the map for a second. "It's not on here anywhere, and these are the most recent charts we have. That planet is not marked on any of them."

A bright grin spread across Diana's face. "You know what that means, don't you?" she asked.

Jacob was smiling as much as Diana was. "We've discovered a new planet!" he whooped. He would have jumped out of his seat, but there wasn't room inside the cockpit. "Let's go down and look around," he said in an excited voice.

"That's just what I was thinking," Diana answered. With a touch of the throttle, the ship edged forward. It swerved and dropped into the planet's atmosphere. Then it skimmed swiftly

A bright grin spread across Diana's face.

just above the ground.

"It's an unusual-looking place," Jacob noted. "I've seen deserts that were more interesting than this."

The planet's surface was perfectly smooth. There was not a hill or a valley to be seen. And the planet didn't seem to have any water at all. For miles, the ground was nothing but a bed of sand.

"Is there any life down there?" Diana asked.

Jacob pressed another group of buttons. A few lights blinked on and off. Then a jumble of letters and numbers spread across the screen. Jacob studied them closely.

"The scanner shows only sand. There may be moisture somewhere in the ground, but there isn't anything living on this planet. The air is fine for breathing, though. We won't need helmets,"

Jacob told her. "Shall we go down?"

"I don't see why not," Diana answered. "Since we found the planet, we might as well be the first people to visit." She cut back the power and steered downward. The ship settled lightly onto the soft, flat sand.

Jacob ran several quick tests on the computer. "Everything checks out. We'll be safe out there."

He and Diana strapped on their survival packs. With a turn of a switch, the hatch door swung open. A metal ladder dropped its feet into the sand.

"Wait!" Jacob yelled as Diana stepped out.

She was startled by his sudden shout. "What is it?"

"We need to celebrate this event. This is our first discovery. We deserve a special treat to mark our success," Jacob

9

The ship settled lightly onto the soft, flat sand.

said. He winked and then sprinted to the back of the ship. He returned with a fat, green watermelon under his arm.

Diana's eyes grew wide. "Where did you get that thing?" she asked.

"I brought it along for a surprise. I smuggled it aboard with the other fruit," said Jacob.

Diana shook her head and chuckled. She climbed down the ladder. Jacob handed her the cold melon and scrambled down after her. Diana put the melon in the shadow of the ship.

The two explorers walked silently in a giant circle. Two suns bathed the planet in bright light. There was no wind, and the only sound was the crunching of sand beneath boots.

"It's beautiful in a strange sort of way," said Jacob.

"But I sure wouldn't want to live

here," Diana added.

Jacob agreed with her. He knelt down and grabbed a handful of sand. The white grains slipped between his fingers. "No wonder nothing grows here," he said. "It's as dry as a bone."

Before long, they were back at the ship. "Let's eat," Diana shouted happily.

The watermelon was still cool. Jacob drew out his knife and cut two thick slices. He gave one to his partner, and they sat down on the sand. He and Diana attacked the sweet, juicy food. It was delicious, and they merrily spat the seeds on the ground. Soon the sand nearby was dotted with the black specks.

The explorers were too busy eating to hear the noise around them. As the seeds hit the ground, they were sprouting roots. The roots were diving deeply into the soil. They were getting power from the strange sand.

All at once, a melon vine shot along the ground. It ran as fast as a streak of lightning. Jacob and Diana jumped to their feet. Around them, vines were racing everywhere over the sand. And new sprouts were coming up each second. One twisted up Diana's arm like a snake.

"What's going on?" Jacob cried.

"I don't know, but we've got to get out of here now!" Diana answered. She jerked the vine off her sleeve, but before she could move, another one slithered around her ankle.

"The ship!" cried Diana. Jacob wheeled around and stared wide-eyed.

The ship was covered with the green vines. The whole planet had become an instant jungle. The growing plants shook the ground with earthquake force. The vines were now as big as trees, and melons were the size of cars and houses. The weight of the plants crushed the ship. Its metal hull crinkled like paper.

"Watch out!" Jacob screamed. A huge melon was rolling heavily toward them. Jacob yanked Diana out of its way. The melon hit a thick growth of vines and stopped. There was a narrow space still open, and the explorers dove into a passage.

Jacob and Diana stood in an empty patch within the tangle of vines. More small vines tried to grow shoots, but they cut them back with their lasers. The spreading plants made horrible sounds like screaming animals. Then suddenly, it all stopped as fast as it had started.

Diana and Jacob waited in the passage. Outside, it was deathly quiet.

"What happened?" Jacob asked.

"It must be over. The soil must be dead now. There's not enough food in it to grow any more plants," Diana guessed.

Jacob fired his pistol at the wall of vines ahead of him. The ruby-colored beam burned through the plants. Jacob aimed his laser to carve a tunnel to open ground. Diana crawled out after him.

Above, they could barely see the sky between the giant leaves. Slowly they cut their way toward the ship. When they found it, Diana sighed loudly. It was flattened, and it would never fly again.

"What did you say about not wanting to live here?" asked Jacob. He smiled weakly.

Diana took a small box out of her pack. She pulled up its antenna and turned a switch. The transmitter began to beep

Jacob sliced a gigantic melon with his laser.

steadily. It would take the rescue party some time to follow the signal.

"There is one thing to be glad about," Jacob said.

"And what's that?" groaned Diana.

Jacob sliced a gigantic melon with his laser. The fruit was as big as a boulder. "We have plenty of food. But watch where you spit your seeds."

A Deadly Shower

Chuck adjusted the dial on the pitching machine. Then he walked quickly back across the yard. The bright gravel that covered the ground crunched under his feet. He picked up his metal bat and held it high. With his thumb, he pressed the button on the bat.

The pitching machine whirred to life. Chuck eyed the hole in the center of it. The first ball came out low and fast. Chuck swung hard with the feather-light bat and hit the ball solidly. The ball rocketed out to the right. It would have gone a long way. But suddenly, the machine made a shrill noise. The ball halted in midair. Then it flew straight to the "pitcher." With this toy, Chuck never had to chase a ball.

After ten more pitches, Chuck paused to rest. The pale blue sun was quite hot, and the only shade was inside the house. There were no plants on this planet. It was the strangest outpost Chuck had ever lived on.

He wiped the sweat off his face. The air suddenly felt cooler on his brow.

Chuck stared at the horizon. The sky was clear and empty. He quickly spun

*Chuck stared at the horizon. The sky was
clear and empty.*

around on his feet and checked in all directions. But there was nothing new to see.

Then he heard the faint wail of a distant siren. Another siren went off closer to him. In seconds, sirens were blaring from all sides. The air was suddenly bitter cold.

The bat fell with a clatter from the boy's hands. His feet slipped on the sparkling gravel as he ran. Wildly, he sprinted for the house. The air grew colder with each step, and Chuck's breath began to form white clouds. His heart throbbed inside his chest.

Without stopping, Chuck glanced back over his shoulder. Ahead of him, the sky was still clear. But behind, it was ablaze with a million bits of flashing colors. There were bright reds, blues, greens and, mostly, whites and silvers. They all churned and boiled in the racing cloud that was coming at Chuck like a flying monster.

Chuck turned his eyes forward. The house was still twenty yards off. He saw his mother holding the door wide open.

"Faster, Chuck!" she yelled. "Run as fast as you can!"

Click. The first crystal hit the ground at Chuck's heels. *Click . . . click, click . . . click, click, click, click.* They began to fall like clear bullets from the sky. They sliced the air with an evil swish.

One hit Chuck's shoulder as he dove for the doorway. It cut through his shirt like a tiny razor. Chuck felt it dig into his skin. He landed on the porch, head-first. The boy tumbled through the door past his mother and lay gasping on the floor.

Chuck's mother bent over him. "Are

Chuck landed on the porch headfirst.

you all right?" she asked. "Did any of them hit you?"

Chuck was too out of breath to answer. He shifted onto his stomach. A spot of blood was soaking through a small hole in his shirt.

"That's not too bad, thank goodness," his mother said. She helped her son to his feet. He took off his shirt and sat in a chair by the window. His mother went to get a pair of tweezers.

"You were lucky," she said when she came back. She brought some iodine with the tweezers. "What if you had tripped or something?"

"They usually don't come up that fast," Chuck panted.

He leaned forward and gritted his teeth as his mother poured iodine on the wound. Then she grabbed the tiny crystal with the tweezers. It came out smoothly, but his shoulder still hurt. Chuck's hands were clenched into tight fists. The iodine burned inside the cut.

"There, that will take care of it," she said. She handed Chuck the crystal and stuck on a bandage. "Now, Chuck, promise me you'll wear your storm jacket next time you go outside."

"I will," Chuck answered. He sat back in the chair and gazed out the window. Crystals showered from the sky in silvery sheets. They bounced like hailstones as they hit the ground.

The storms meant death to anyone caught outside. The crystal edges were hard and sharp. And the clouds spat them down like machine guns. But from inside, the storms were the most beautiful things Chuck had ever seen. The air sparkled like a shattered rainbow. The sun was a broken blue ball shining through the storm. Chuck looked at the stone in his hand. It gleamed and flashed even under the indoor light.

The tick of the crystals hitting the windows soon grew softer. The storm was letting up. There were already three inches of the glassy stones on the ground. At last, the house was still. Once more, the air was as warm as a summer's day, and the sky was perfectly clear.

Chuck stood up and put on his shirt. He was almost out the door when his mother called.

"Don't forget to clear the back walk, too. The vacuum won't be by until tomorrow," she said.

"I know," Chuck answered. He went to the storage shed and found the shovel. He dragged it behind him to the end of the walk. The broad, metal blade clanged

*Chuck dragged the shovel behind him to
the end of the walk.*

over the icelike gravel.

In the distance, Chuck heard the hum of the vacuums. They were sucking up the crystals at the far end of town. Chuck laughed to himself.

Those people on Earth must be crazy, he thought. *Why would anyone want these annoying things?*

He threw the first scoop of diamonds off the walk.

Field Trip

John gulped down the last of his orange juice. He glanced at the clock and turned back to the newspaper. There was still one comic strip he hadn't read. He didn't even look up when his sister came into the kitchen.

"You'd better not fool around," Kim

said. "You'll be late for school today."

"I know, I know," John said, still reading his paper. When he finished, he dropped his dishes in the cleaning tube, then raced down the hall without a book, paper, or pen.

"Watch the computer," Kim called after him. "It's been acting strangely lately."

John opened the door to a room in the back of the house. It was like the cockpit of an airplane at night. There was one chair in the center of the floor, with rows of blinking lights and switches around it. There were no windows, and the room was dark except for the tiny lights. It took a minute for John's eyes to adjust. He sat down in the soft, fat chair and leaned back. He had made it to school on time.

"Good morning, John," said a metallic voice. "Did you sleep well last night?"

*"Watch the computer," Kim called after John.
"It's been acting strange lately."*

"Just fine, thank you," the student answered.

"I'm glad to hear that," the computer said. "Let's start with math first today. In our last lesson, we were adding fractions."

A panel opened in the wall in front of John. Behind it was a keyboard like a typewriter that John would use to punch in his answers.

Each problem was displayed on a TV screen. John moved his fingers over the keys. New numbers came up on the screen.

For the next hour, the computer drilled John on math. It praised him when he got something right, and it explained his errors. Its voice was soft and kind, but there was always a slight metal ring to it.

After the math lesson, the computer

Each problem was displayed on a TV screen.

turned to science. Then came English. Finally, the computer gave John a quiz in history. John was glad he had studied. He answered all of the questions with ease.

"You have done well," the computer said.

"Thanks," said the student.

"And as a surprise, I've planned a field trip today. I'm sending you back to the age of dinosaurs. You'll recall we studied them last week," the computer noted. "Please place your hands on the sensor pads."

There was a hump on each arm of the chair. John put his hands on them, palms down. His skin began to tingle. There was a ringing in his head, and suddenly, the walls of the room disappeared.

John was standing alone in the middle of a jungle. The air was hot and damp.

The boy's shirt began to stick to his skin. He was quickly soaked with sweat.

Around him, the world was a rich green. Huge trees towered over him. The shorter plants had fat, shiny leaves. Some leaves were as big as doors. The thick moss on the ground was soft and spongy. John was tempted to take off his shoes.

He began walking through the jungle. He recalled what he had learned about this era of time. He knew he wouldn't see men here. But he could hardly wait to find a dinosaur.

John pushed his way through the leaves. Ahead, he could hear the sound of running water. The heat had built up his thirst.

John stepped out onto the bank of a wide stream. He gasped and his heart skipped a beat. A giant crocodile glided away from the bank. Suddenly, John had a shocking thought. He was nothing special here. There were plenty of animals larger than he. And he would make a tasty meal for many of them. He would have to be careful.

With a watchful eye, John bent down to drink. All at once, he heard a crashing sound behind him. Something large and heavy was coming his way. John began to run along the bank of the stream. He looked back over his shoulder.

A huge, gray head poked through the leaves. It was at least twelve feet off the ground. It looked up and down the stream. And when it saw John, the animal charged out into the open.

John had wanted to see a dinosaur. But he hadn't wanted to be this close. The dinosaur was standing on its back feet. Its huge body was covered with a tough, leathery skin. Its mouth was filled with sharp, jagged teeth. Hissing, the dinosaur began to chase after John. The ground shook beneath the running monster.

John looked back again. The beast was gaining on him fast. On open ground, John didn't stand a chance. He cut back through the dense jungle. The dinosaur turned right behind him.

In terror, the boy fought his way through the plants. Sharp leaves smacked him in the face. But he didn't dare stop. The dinosaur was still after him. He could hear it smashing through the jungle.

All of a sudden, the ground grew muddier. John was in the middle of a small clearing. The mud was up to his ankles, and he began to sink deeper. He tried to pull his foot out of the gritty goo, but it

John looked back again. The beast was gaining on him fast.

was held in tightly. The mud was now up to his knees.

"Quicksand!" he screamed.

John looked around for something to grab. There was nothing in reach, and he could no longer move his legs. The mud was sucking him down steadily. In no time, it was around his waist.

Then John saw the dinosaur. It was watching him from the edge of the mud-hole. It knew better than to come after him.

John struggled to get out. But his movements only made him sink faster. Finally, he was too tired to fight. The quicksand was up to his neck. In seconds, it would smother him. John tilted his head back for one last breath.

"HELP!" he shouted at the top of his lungs, and everything went black.

"Did you enjoy your field trip?" asked

the computer.

John's eyes flew open. He was sitting in the classroom, but he was still panting. And his heart was still racing.

"That was *too* real!" John answered.

"I'll keep that in mind," the computer said. "That's all for the day. Don't forget your homework."

Wearily, John left the classroom. Kim was waiting in the hall for her turn.

John went to his room to take a shower. He felt as if he had run a long race. The thought of the dinosaur made him shiver.

"It was just too real," he mumbled. He pulled off his shoes. Then he noticed something strange. There was mud in the tread of his shoe. And it was still soft and wet.

John bolted down the hall like a bullet. His scream echoed through the house. *"Kim, don't go in there!"*

Home Run, Three Miles

"What do you do around here for fun?" Sue asked. She followed Tucker down a long hall. He was carrying Sue's suitcases to the guest bedroom.

"The same things you do back on Earth," Tucker laughed.

Sue wasn't sure she could believe her cousin. She glanced out the windows of the life-pod. The world outside looked too cold and hard to enjoy. She could see mountains of stone many miles in the distance. There were no clouds to block her view, because this planet had no air. The gravity here wasn't strong enough to hold an atmosphere.

"Did you bring your baseball glove?" Tucker asked. "I mentioned it in my last letter. I remembered that you are a great baseball fan."

"I brought it," Sue answered. "But I don't see how we'll get a chance to use it. We can't throw here in the hall."

"Are you kidding?" Tucker asked with a wise smile. "This is the greatest planet in the universe for baseball. We never have to worry about the weather."

"That's because you don't have any,"

Sue glanced out the windows of the life-pod.

Sue joked with a laugh.

"Well, just hurry up and unpack. I've got a baseball game set up for three o'clock, and you're playing in left field with me," said Tucker. He set her luggage in the bedroom and flexed his tired arms. "But don't bother unpacking your cleats," he said as he left.

A while later, Tucker yelled down the hall. "Let's go! It's almost three!"

Sue hurried to meet her cousin in the living room. Like Tucker, she was wearing a jersey and sweat pants. Her glove was stuck on her left hand.

"Are we really going to play outside?" she asked.

"You've got it," Tucker laughed. He handed her a suit made out of a thin, silver plastic. It was one piece from toe to neck. There were even gloves sewn onto the ends of the sleeves. It seemed

funny to Sue to be wearing a glove inside her baseball glove.

Tucker placed a helmet over her head
and hooked it to the suit. Then he flicked
a switch at the base of the helmet. At
once, Sue felt fresh air flowing through
the suit. She looked at Tucker through
the dark lens of the helmet. When he
had his on, she heard a click beside her
ears. Tucker's voice came through clearly
on the helmet's speaker. The two players
left the life-pod.

At first, Sue had trouble walking. She
felt so light in the planet's weak gravity
that she moved like a crazy, bouncing
ball after Tucker. They went to a rocky
desert beyond the life-pods. A group
of kids was already there. In just a
minute, the teams were chosen. Tucker
and Sue headed out into left field. They
walked and walked before Tucker finally

45

At first, Sue had trouble walking.

stopped. The other players were just tiny dots far in the distance.

"It might take you a few minutes to catch on," Tucker said. "Batting is the same as on Earth. But since we have so little gravity, the ball will really sail. A good home run will travel about three miles. We're about two and a half miles from home plate right now."

"I can barely see the players. How will I ever see the ball?" asked Sue.

"Oh, you'll see it all right. It's a special ball," Tucker told her. "This is a fielder's game — and a game of home runs. I'll be playing about half a mile to your right." He bounded off over the rocks.

"O.K., is everyone ready?" said a voice. It was the pitcher talking.

"Ready," each player answered.

"Burn one by him," Sue heard Tucker add. She climbed upon a nearby boulder

47

for a better view. She could hardly make out the infield players.

"Here we go," said the pitcher. Suddenly, there was a bright flash at the plate. "It's a hit," screamed the pitcher. "It looks like a two-miler at least."

Sue saw a glowing green dot sailing toward right field. It flew high and long, like a strange shooting star. Then it began to drop back to the ground.

"I've got it; I've got it," the right fielder said over the radio. Sue couldn't even see him, but she heard the thump of the ball landing in his glove. Then the green dot was flying back toward the plate. Now Sue understood the game here. And she couldn't wait for someone to hit something to her. She was charged with excitement.

Within seconds, there was another flash at the plate. Sue squinted hard. At first, the green dot didn't seem to be moving. Then she realized that it was coming right toward her.

"It's a short one. Move in on it," Tucker radioed. Sue didn't think she could reach it in time. Forgetting where she was, she leaped off the boulder. In the weak gravity, she flew twenty feet in one jump. She was shocked by how far she could hop. Each step pushed her high in the air, but she came down like a feather. It was almost a mile to the ball. She covered the distance in no time. In fact, her last jump carried her in too far. The ball flew over her and hit the ground.

"Throw it in!" Tucker yelled. Sue scrambled after the green light. It glowed brightly under a rock. Sue picked it up and looked to the infield. Home plate was over a mile away. Could she throw it that far?

She cocked her arm and hurled the ball. It took off like a satellite through the sky. She wasn't exactly sure where it went. But, over the radio, the pitcher told her it had been a good throw. Smiling, Sue bounded back to her boulder.

The next pitch brought another slam Sue's way. "This one's going long!" cried Tucker.

Sue moved back in broad, high hops. She watched the green dot over her shoulder. It was coming down too fast for her to get under it. She had just one chance.

Sue turned and faced the approaching light. Just before it passed over her, she leaped straight up into the sky. With her glove above her head, she shot up as high as a house. Her timing couldn't have been better. The ball hit squarely in her glove.

Sue leaped straight up into the sky.

"Fantastic!" Tucker howled over the radio.

"I'll never be content with Earth baseball again," Sue laughed.

"If you get tired of this, we can go play on Planet Seven. Their gravity is much stronger than Earth's," said Tucker. "A good hit there is twenty feet."

"No, thanks," Sue answered. "It's easier to be a star here." She hurled the ball back toward the infield. It made the three-mile flight in just one bounce.

Cosmic Net

A large crowd of people was waiting by the launching tube. Nearly everyone on the space station was there. They talked in hushed voices.

"Here he comes now," someone shouted. All eyes peered down the hall. The crowd began to cheer as Greg walked.

"Here he comes now," someone shouted.

toward them. He was dressed in a silvery space suit. In his hand, he carried a polished, white helmet.

Greg waved and stepped into the launching tube. "Find something great," he heard someone call to him.

That's exactly what Greg was setting out to do. He had stopped at this space port to pick up supplies. From here, he would fly into uncharted space. He was a seeker of new worlds.

Before boarding, Greg walked once around his ship. Everything seemed to be in good shape. He climbed into the cockpit and sealed the door. Outside, the crew cleared the launching area.

A green light flashed on the control panel. With a touch of Greg's hand, the ship blasted into space. In a few minutes, the space station was just a speck on the radar screen.

Greg flicked some buttons. He gave signals to the computer. Then he relaxed in his seat and closed his eyes. The ship would fly itself until it reached uncharted space. From then on, Greg would fly it. Then the computer would make new maps and run tests. The pilot slept soundly as the miles went by.

Greg woke up to the sound of a buzzer. The ship was slowing down smoothly. He sat up and threw a switch. A map appeared on the viewer. There was a lone dot blinking on the edge of the screen. That was the ship's position. The computer had no maps of the space ahead. With a smile, Greg took over the controls, and the ship entered the unknown.

The next few hours dragged by slowly. There was little of interest to look at. The computer whirred as it made up new charts.

Greg glanced at the radar screen. Only one dark planet was anywhere close by. *I may as well check it out,* he thought.

Greg hit a button, and the ship veered off to the right. He pushed it on to top speed. Then he left to get something to eat from the storeroom.

Suddenly, the ship slammed to a complete halt. Greg was thrown forward through the cabin. He crashed into his control seat.

A dozen buzzers went off at once. The instrument panel was filled with flashing red lights. Greg stumbled to his feet and plopped over in the seat. His side was aching from his fall, and a bump was growing on his head.

Quickly, he shut down the engines. The warning lights went out, one by one. When the last buzzer was silent, Greg glanced out the window.

"What in the world...?" he gasped.

He closed his eyes, shook his head, and then looked out again. He still couldn't believe what he was seeing.

The ship was tangled up in some kind of net. The strands of the net were no thicker than a finger. That's why the radar hadn't picked them up. Greg looked up and down, left and right. The net seemed to stretch forever in all directions.

"I can't let this stop me," he whispered.

Greg's fingers danced over a row of switches. The ship's engines started up with a roar. Greg shifted them to full power. The ship shuddered under the mighty force. But it couldn't break the silky net.

After a minute, Greg threw the engines into reverse. The net stretched as the craft strained to back away. But the

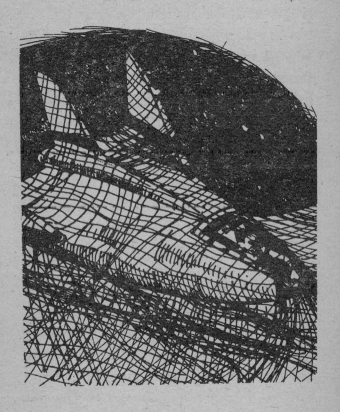

The ship was tangled up in some kind of net.

ship was held tight. Greg shut off the power and sat quietly in the dark cabin.

Well, there's just one thing to do, he thought. Leaving his seat, he put on his helmet. He found the power saw in the storeroom. Finally, he hooked the power lines and jet pack to his suit. With a hum, the ship's door slid open. Greg stepped out into space.

He floated a few yards away from the ship. Even from out here, the net seemed to have no end. Greg looked over at the dark planet.

I didn't realize I was so close to it, he thought. *It must be caught in the net, too.*

Using the jet pack, he flew back to the net. He squeezed the handle of the saw, and the blade began spinning. Greg pressed it against a strand of the net and cut through the strange fiber. A minute later, the strand snapped in two.

*Greg pressed the blade against
a strand of the net.*

Greg floated on to the next nearest one. He worked hard to free the ship, but it was a slow job. After cutting three more strands, he stopped to rest. He glanced at the dark planet. It seemed larger and nearer than before. But Greg knew that was impossible.

Suddenly, the entire net shook wildly. Greg was knocked backwards, but his power line caught him. His eyes were drawn by a movement near the dark planet, then they stretched wide with terror. The planet had legs and eyes! It was creeping along the net toward the ship.

A long, black tongue flickered out of its mouth. The stellar spider reached for its prey with its huge pincer. Greg's scream was lost in the silence of space.

Planet of Stone

With care, Karen pinched a dead leaf off one of her plants. The whole window was filled with greenery. The plants were her pets, and they went with her on each long voyage. They kept her from getting too homesick.

"What's our next stop?" Karen asked.

"Planet Three-one-four," said Jack, who was sitting at the controls of the small spaceship. "We'll be there in a few hours."

"Is there anything interesting about it?" Karen asked.

"No, there's no life on the planet," he told her. "But there is plenty of air and water. In many ways, it's a lot like Earth. That's why we're supposed to run some tests there. The chief wants to know why it has no life."

"The chief should come out here and see for himself. We've been out too long. I'm tired of doing these planet studies. I wish he'd call us in," Karen sighed. She and her partner had been on this assignment for ten weeks.

"I think this will be the last stop," smiled Jack, "because this is the last of the new planets on the chart." He was as ready as Karen to fly home.

"I hope so," Karen said. "My plants aren't doing too well on the ship's water. It's too pure or something." She pulled another brown leaf off a fern.

"It tastes flat, too," Jack agreed.

The ship sailed silently through space. A while later, Jack spotted planet Three-one-four. It looked like a faint star at first, but as the miles sped by, Three-one-four grew larger. Finally, it appeared much like Earth—a blue ball frosted with white clouds.

Karen took her seat beside Jack at the controls. She always did the takeoffs and landings. She had a smoother touch on the control buttons.

The ship dove like a bullet through the atmosphere, then it skimmed just over a mountain range. At last, the ship's computer chose a place to land, and the craft settled on the ground with

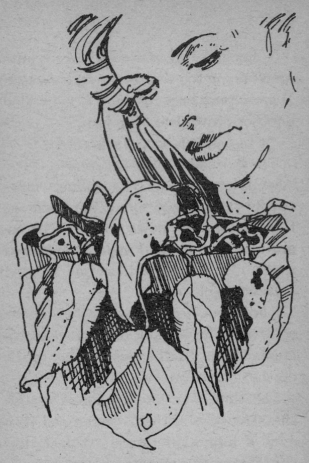

Karen said, "My plants aren't doing
too well on the ship's water."

hardly a bump.

Jack was already standing at the door. He carried a pack of equipment on each shoulder. "Open," he said into a grill in the wall. The door opened smoothly, and a ramp unfolded to the ground.

Karen went to the back of the ship to get her own pack. When she returned, Jack was still at the door. His mouth was hanging open like a broken hatch. "Well, what are you waiting for?" Karen asked.

She peered out over Jack's shoulder. Suddenly, her jaw dropped just like his, and her eyes widened. For a second, both explorers were speechless.

Before them was a landscape just like something on Earth. There were trees, bushes, and meadows of grass. But even though a warm breeze was blowing, nothing was moving. Everything was

The door opened smoothly, and a ramp unfolded to the ground.

made of stone.

"It's unbelievable," Karen said.

"And beautiful," Jack added.

Together they edged down the ramp. When he reached the end, Jack stuck out his foot. Blades of grass snapped with a clinking sound beneath his shoe. His tracks were as clear as if he had been walking in the snow.

Carefully, he walked to a nearby tree. He broke off a leaf and looked at it closely. It was the perfect twin of a leaf on Earth. But even though it was as thin as paper, it was hard and brittle. And its color was not green, but the blue-gray of stone.

"This will sure get the chief excited," said Jack, as he stuck the leaf in his pack. "Let's go ahead and start the tests. We can explore while the machines are running."

Eagerly, Jack and Karen went to work. They set up the equipment beside the ship. Jack ran a power cable out from the door. Karen set the gauges to their proper settings. With a flick of a switch, the machines began ticking and humming.

"That does it," Karen called. "Let's head down through those woods."

"Those aren't woods—those are stones," Jack laughed.

The pair walked slowly through the rock-trees. Every pine needle was now a sharp sliver of stone that could cut through their shoes. They took extra care not to trip.

"I see something moving up there," Jack said, pointing to something sparkling through the stone-brush.

"It's a spring," Karen answered. They pushed their way to a pool of water.

Drops were trickling down over some rocks.

Jack tested the water with a color tablet. "It's good," he said.

Karen pulled out an empty jar and filled it up. "This is just what my plants need," she said. "I'll be back in a minute." She crunched through the woods back to the ship.

Careful not to spill a drop, Karen watered her dry plants. She tried to give each one the same amount. The real plants looked so green compared to what was outside. To her, green was much better than slate-gray At last, the jar was empty.

As Karen turned to go out for a refill, her elbow barely hit one of the pots on the shelf. Karen heard the crash behind her. She looked around, expecting to see a broken pot on the floor, but the pot

*Jack tried to raise his arm, but it was
already too stiff.*

was still in one solid piece. Instead, the top of the plant was broken off. And it was shattered into a hundred pieces.

Karen picked up one of the leaves. Already it was as hard as stone. Before her eyes, it turned from green to gray. She bolted out the door and down the trail.

"Jack! Hey, Jack! You'll never believe what happened," she cried. "The chief is going to love this."

Suddenly, Karen stopped in the path. Her face became deathly white. A scream rolled out between the fingers covering her mouth. It echoed over the stony landscape.

Jack tried to raise his arm, but it was already too stiff. He was kneeling by the spring. His drinking cup was clutched in his hand. The tips of his fingers were slate-gray.

Green Doctor

The doctor took the thermometer from Glenda's lips. He held the glass rod up to the light. His eyes strained as he read the small numbers.

"Well, how bad is her fever?" said the tall woman standing by the bed. There was worry and fear in her voice. She

74

"Well, how bad is her fever?"

looked back and forth from her daughter to the doctor.

"No better, no worse, Anne," sighed the doctor. He laid the thermometer on the table by the bed. His hand then closed around the girl's wrist. Softly, he counted the beats of her pulse.

Anne went into a sudden rage. "I knew it!" she cried. "I knew we shouldn't have come to this planet! There's nothing good here! There's nothing but vines that don't grow! And the nearest hospital is a week's flight away!"

She stared angrily out the window for a few seconds. Then she burst into tears. Her husband, Tim, moved to comfort her.

"Coming here had nothing to do with Glenda's getting sick. And the care she'll get here is just as good as anywhere else. She'll be fine in a few days," he said.

Hugging his wife, Tim looked sadly

out the window. There were a few trees. But mostly, only vines covered the ground. They were strange plants. They were alive, but they never grew. Tim had come here to study them.

"Tim's right," said the doctor. "Glenda came in contact with the disease before she came here. It's just now starting to hit her. It's popping up all over the galaxy. And even the best experts haven't found a cure yet. Glenda may as well be here as anywhere else."

The doctor filled a long needle with a green fluid. Glenda didn't even flinch when he stuck it in her arm. Her eyes were barely open, and her face was flushed. Her breathing was weak and shallow.

"The shot may keep the fever from getting worse," he said. "I'll stop back in the morning." Glenda's parents followed the doctor out of the room.

With a tired, blank stare, Glenda gazed out the window. She wasn't in pain, but she could hardly move. There was no energy left in her body. Slowly, her eyelids began to droop.

Then from somewhere, Glenda heard a scratching noise. It was very faint, and it seemed far off in the distance. The sick girl forced her eyes open. She couldn't believe what she saw.

The noise wasn't coming from far away at all. As she watched, a vine grew slowly up the screen in her window. Like the minute hand of a clock, it was barely moving. But if she looked closely, she could see it climbing. The shoot made a sliding sound as it stretched over the screen. She wanted to tell someone about it, but she was too sleepy.

Glenda awoke four hours later. At

once, she turned her head toward the window. Now there were five or six vines on the screen. They twisted and crossed each other to form a green net. Again, Glenda could hear them sliding over the screen as they grew.

Glenda didn't even have the strength to call out. She waited until her mother came into the bedroom. Anne carried a bowl of soup on a tray.

Glenda's arm felt like a lead weight as she pointed to the window. When Anne glanced at the screen, she gasped in shock. The tray tumbled from her hands. The bowl shattered loudly on the floor.

"Tim, come quickly! The vines are growing!" she cried.

Glenda's father sprinted down the hall. He thought something must be wrong with his daughter. Then he caught sight of the vine-covered screen. Like the rest of the family, he was stunned by what he saw.

"The lab," he whispered in amazement. "I've got to get them to the lab." He ran outside like a madman. In minutes, he was digging up the plants outside the window. They didn't seem to want to let go of the screen. He had to jerk hard to get them loose. Soon, he was taking his prize down to his laboratory.

Glenda was too tired to eat. When she woke up again, the sun was just setting. She could hear her parents in the other room.

"I don't understand it, Anne," Tim was saying. "They just quit growing when I got them in the lab."

And with his voice, Glenda could hear another sound. There was a scraping noise outside her window. She watched numbly as a single vine sprout climbed

*Tim was digging up the plants
outside the window.*

to the edge of the screen. It was growing quickly. It moved much faster than the others had. It crawled up and down, back and forth across the screen.

The vine swelled until it was as thick as a snake. It now covered every inch of the window. The thin metal screen began to snap under the weight. The vine was pushing to get inside. The screen gave way in a screech of metal.

The plant raced across the floor toward the bed. It was growing an inch a second. Glenda was too weak to roll away. She saw her parents running down the hall. Anne screamed in terror and tried to reach Glenda. But she was held back by Tim.

All three of them watched as the vine twisted up the bedpost. It shot across the sheet toward Glenda's arm. When the plant touched her skin, it stopped

All three of them watched as the vine twisted up the bedpost.

growing for a second. Then, ever so slowly, a thin sprout wrapped itself around the girl's wrist. Tiny thorns began to grow along the sprout. As the vine thickened, the thorns cut deep into Glenda's skin. But no blood dripped onto the white sheets. It was sucked into the vine through the thorns.

Suddenly, the rope-like plant quivered. Then it started to turn brown and shrivel up. At the same time, Glenda felt energy pour through her body. In seconds, she was jumping out of bed. The vine was dead and dry on the floor. Glenda ran to her weeping mother's arms.

Her father dashed out of the room. In minutes, he was shouting over the radio to the doctor. "I don't care what diseases they have—just get them to this planet," Tim cried with joy.

New Earth

"Last flight for New Earth leaving in one hour! Last flight for New Earth leaving in one hour!" The voice boomed out over the city. It was loud enough to shake the windows of Trish's room.

There was a lot of other noise in the building, too. People were running up and down the steps with loaded arms, their suitcases jammed full. They didn't want to leave anything behind. Once they were gone, they could never return. It would take years just to reach New Earth.

Trish threw her last coat in her suitcase. Her closet stood open and bare. Most of her things were already on the spaceship. She looked around the room for anything she might have forgotten. Leaving her room made her a little sad. But she couldn't wait around. She still had to pick up Old Man.

Trish hauled her heavy suitcase down the hall. Nearly everyone was on board the ship already, but some people were running late, as she was. No one offered to help her carry her luggage. She dragged it down the steps and out on the sidewalk.

*People were running up and down the steps
with loaded arms.*

The streets had never looked so lonely. The few skimmers parked by the curb were loaded down. Still, their owners were trying to stuff more into them. Trish was glad she had just one bag to carry.

Quickly, she hefted it into the back of her skimmer, then she hopped into the driver's seat and zoomed off. She didn't like to drive so fast. But there was barely enough time to pick up Old Man and board the ship.

The traffic grew thicker near the launch site. Trish hoped it would thin out before she returned with Old Man. She cut down an alley and sped away from the traffic.

Above the purr of the skimmer, Trish could hear the warnings. "Last flight for New Earth leaving in thirty minutes!"

Trish drove a bit faster over the

concrete slab. For as far as she could see, there was nothing but cement buildings and parking lots. There were no lawns or trees. They had all been dug up, cut down, and paved over. Millions of empty skimmers were parked on miles of concrete.

Trish drove into a neighborhood of small houses. All of the yards were slabs of white cement. The houses were the same white color—except one. Old Man's house could be seen from blocks away. It was painted a rich, emerald green. Everyone laughed at it. They said Old Man was a little crazy. Trish even wondered herself, but she loved him like a father. She drove over the slab right up to the door.

"Old Man, are you ready to go?" Trish called. She got out of the skimmer and beat on the door. "Are you ready? The

89

*Trish drove into a neighborhood
of small houses.*

ship for New Earth will be leaving in just a few minutes."

No one answered her. Then Trish heard a clinking sound in back of the house. She rushed around to find her strange friend. "There you are," she said with a smile.

Old Man was standing in the middle of the "yard" with a pick in his hands. There was a shovel lying close by. He saw Trish but kept on swinging the pick. Its sharp point chipped away at the concrete. Large chunks of cement were scattered about the slab. There was black-brown dirt in the hole he dug. Old Man stopped to wipe his brow.

"What are you doing, Old Man?" Trish asked.

"Digging," he answered simply.

"Well, I won't ask why now. We don't have time to talk. The ship is taking off in minutes, and with millions of people on board, they won't wait for the two of us. I hope you've packed your suitcases," she said.

Old Man turned to look at the space-ship. His eyes gazed out through the thick, polluted air. The ship was miles away, but it still seemed huge. It was the largest thing humans had ever built. It would carry the people of Earth to a planet far across the galaxy. New Earth, the place was called. There was no pollution there. Old Man suddenly swung his pick at the cement with new strength.

"Put that down and let's go," Trish said, grabbing the sleeve of his shirt.

Old Man stared straight at Trish. His eyes were hard and honest. Trish had never seen such force in them before. "I'm not going," he said calmly.

Trish laughed nervously. "Of course

you're going," she said. She tried to pull Old Man by the arm, but she couldn't budge him an inch.

"I'm not going," he repeated.

Then Trish saw that he wasn't kidding. Her heart sank at the thought of losing the dearest person in her life. Tears flooded her eyes. "You've got to go," she cried. "New Earth will be beautiful. It will be clean and covered with plants and trees. You can have a garden in your backyard."

"For how long?" Old Man mumbled. He broke off a block of cement and threw it aside. The patch of dirt was growing bigger with each swing of the pick.

Trish looked from her friend to the ship. Then with a sob, she threw her arms around Old Man's neck. "You can't stay here alone."

He held her gently while she cried. All

of a sudden, the ground shook wildly. The roar of an explosion blasted their ears. The whole sky was filled with flaming light. In the distance, the great ship rose into the sky.

Trish and Old Man watched it fly out of sight. Black smoke trailed from its giant engines. And a final load of garbage fell from its trash ports.

"I've missed it!" Trish screamed. "I've missed it!" She dropped to her knees and cried painfully. Quietly, Old Man left her and went into his house. She didn't even notice when he came back. All she heard was the sound of his shovel in the dirt.

When she opened her swollen eyes, Trish saw a tree. It was only inches tall, but it was green and healthy. Carefully, Old Man pulled it from its pot. He planted it lovingly in the hole he had dug.

Old Man planted the tree lovingly
in the hole he had dug.

Old Man placed Trish's hand in his own. "This is New Earth," he said softly. "They took the old one with them."

The idea swept the sorrow from Trish's heart like cool, clean water.